Even

To anyone and everyone that takes the time to read this, thank you.

The Hunter, The Wanderer, and The Wolf

He had buried the kill; the fire was high now and burning faster than he had expected. The hunter rose from beside the flames to search for more dry wood, before the snows set in. The dark was deep tonight; there was no moon, only the quiet that slowly settles before a great snow, as nature braces for it to come. Gathering the gnarled branches that he needed was difficult and slow, and it felt as if every step the hunter took offended the icy silence. Still, he persisted, and when he felt satisfied his haul would last the night, he returned to the light.

There was a man at the fire.

He was seated and did not rise when the hunter approached. The man, a wanderer, looked old and worn, cloaked in heavy dark furs and tanned leathers. In his thin, spotted hands he clutched an ash wood walking staff. His face was lit by the flames of the fire and the hunter could see he was old, his gray and white hair knotted in braids. He met the hunter's gaze with one cold gray eye, but the other was sunken and looked like it had been taken a long time ago. The wanderer smiled and spoke in a plain, steady voice. "Can I share your fire tonight?"

The hunter did not hesitate, as if this were not an unexpected encounter deep amongst the trees in the forest. "You are welcome here," he said, "The snows come tonight and the nearest hearth is days from us."

The wanderer smiled; a wolf howled long and cold into the night.

The fire was lower and the snows had begun to fall in gentle flurries in the cold trees around them. The hunter rose and carefully pulled the kill he had prepared earlier from its place in the ground, dusting earth from the lean, flame-charred flesh. The wanderer watched, silent. "Here, a fox snared this morning. It is not much, but it cooked well." The hunter passed his guest a whole haunch and set a dark clay mug in the snow between them.

Another howl, closer.

The hunter filled the mug with the thick mead from his pack and passed it to the wanderer, who took it graciously.

"I did not ask for food and drink. You are kind to share." His gray eye held the hunter's gaze for a moment, and he took a long draft from the mug in his hands.

"I am glad to have the company, I had not expected to see anyone for days." The hunter pulled a fresh piece of wood onto the fire, and they ate and drank their fill as the snow fell ever harder. The forest made sounds of protest, cracking and groaning as something forced itself through the thickets in the dark. A feeling of dread preceded the beast.

Suddenly there was a burst of movement in the dark around them. The pair rose, their backs to the fire as the movement and sounds circled closer. Shining eyes gleamed through the night. "Wolves", the hunter said calmly as he bent to grab a still-burning branch from the fire.

"Wolf", said the wanderer. "Just one."

The bright eyes of the wolf slid in and out of view through the shadowy tree line. Its hulking shape seemed to morph and weave through the gnarled trunks like smoke; the hunter could not tell how big the beast truly was. In a flash of ivory teeth and matted fur it lunged at them from the dark. Equally fast, the wanderer gripped the hunter and pulled him back just as the hulking, pitch-dark mass leapt past.

"Too big," was all the hunter could stammer as he caught his balance.

Though shaken, the hunter was still determined to fight. He stood back-to-back with the wanderer as the beast circled them. It was hiding no more.

The wolf was giant, more massive than any horse the hunter had ever seen, with fur so dark the firelight seemed to fail around it. Its eyes were wild, a bright radiating yellow, and unblinking. It faced them, lowering its shoulders in anticipation, its huge mouth hanging open in a snarl. Like a stone from a sling, it charged. The wanderer stood fast, and as the beast reared over him, he struck it with the fiery branch. The wolf staggered, but did not retreat. It eyed the wanderer with malice and opened its jaws. The hunter thought it surely meant to bite him clean through.

The wolf lunged. The hunter struck, he had taken up the wanderer's staff and in an instant of instinct plunged it into the wolf's gaping mouth. The beast reared once, choked out a pained snarl, and, in that moment, stood as tall as the trees. Then it fell and was still and silent, dead.

The companions stood over the wolf for a moment, the silence once again between them, then they returned to the fire. It had burned low.

The next morning the hunter rose to find the camp was cleared, the wolf was gone, the wanderer was gone. One set of footprints led off to the north. The hunter gathered his camp and finished his meal from the night before and reflected. Then he set out north, to his cabin, following the footsteps in the snow. It was just past the edge of the forest that the trail ended, the footsteps stopped in one place, then four smaller tracks led on for a pace before they stopped without another trace.

When the hunter made it to his own home two days later, he found two ravens perched on the roof above his door. They were coal black and enormous, and in a silent beat of their great wings they took off before he made it to the doorstep of the cabin.

They left on the step two mysterious and magical things the hunter could never quite explain: a coin of purest gold that every evening would double, along with a wolf's tooth the size of knife that never dulled as long as the hunter lived. They say when he finally died an old and wizened man, the ravens returned for their treasures.

For a Fir Tree

A man sat on his porch at mid-day in the cold, his dog beside. The dog raised his head and sniffed the air. He turned to the man and said,

"The fox is about."

The man said nothing; he watched the snow fall in heavy thick clumps. It was the solstice and the man was set to find and down his fir tree for Saturnalia. He rose and retrieved his axe and sled, as the snow fell harder.

The dog was uneasy.

"I should go with you," he said.

"You should not," said the man. "If you come with me, the fox will ransack and plunder our stores. It's late in the year, we would be done." He stood, and stepped off the porch.

The dog huffed, resigned. He turned twice and laid down to await the man's return.

The man set out; the snow was at his ankles. There was a clearing three furlongs into the wood, a clearing of fir trees still small enough to bring along on his sled.

About the second furlong, the fox appeared in the path ahead, a wicked flame sitting in the snow.

"Cold day," said the fox.

The man said nothing.

The fox continued in a low eager voice as he made way for the man and his sled, whose speed was brisk through the drifts.

"What has you out in this weather, good man?"

The man said nothing. The fox eyed the sled and axe.

"For a fir? All of this for a tree? You should slow your pace if you mean to fell a tree and sled it home all yourself," the fox said.

The man looked at the fox, he said:

"You might help?"

The fox smiled, but made no move to help.

"The clearing is still far; you should take a rest."

The man said nothing.

"I would hate to see you twist and fall so far from… help," said the fox.

The fox did not look like he would mind that at all, though.

The two paced on in silence through the snow. It was up to his calves, falling harder still.

The clearing was ahead. The man pulled his sled aside, handled his axe, and made his way into the firs, their branches all covered in fresh snow.

The fox followed.

It did not take the man long to find a fair fir. He cleared the lower limbs and set to work at the trunk with his axe.

The fox questioned him:

"That one? Are you sure, it hardly seems enough."

The man chopped at the base of the fir, and he said nothing.

"You should slow your cutting," the fox persisted, flicking a snow-laced ear, "do you want your heart to fail?"

He paced this way and that, and paused to sniff the air, before he spoke again.

"You should rest your axe and talk awhile."

The man said nothing.

The tree was downed and the man wrestled it on to the sled, the day was long now. He took his time binding the fir down tight, each knot carefully wound; when satisfied, the man hefted the leads to the sled and set off for home.

The fox followed, eying the knots.

"Such rope work," he said, "But some of these binds seem loose... surely you would hate to lose your fir to such laxness."

The man pulled the sled on; he said nothing.

The snow was to his knees now.

The fox was sudden; in a flash it tried a knot with its sharp teeth, but the binds held fast.

"I suppose they are not as loose as they seem." said the fox, not hiding his frustrations.

A furlong to home and the man stopped, the runners of his sled sinking behind him: an old, freshly felled tree blocked the path.

"Oh no," said the fox, circling the man and his sled now, pushing through the deepening snow.

"Well you can't just leave such a fine fir... but what to do? Not even a man as you are could move that tree."

The man said nothing, he waited, the snow fell harder still.

The fox was delighted, the man was waiting, the day was ending and the light fading.

"Are you cold?" asked the fox. "If you rest here tonight, I might show you another way home tomorrow."

The man said nothing, the snow was halfway up the fallen tree. A few more minutes of silence stretched between them.

"It is still far to your cabin, man. There is a stream for water just in the woods. I can take you there, for you must be thirsty." said the fox.

The man said nothing. The snow had covered the fallen tree, and with a swift movement he hoisted the sled up and over the impasse.

The fox scowled.

The light of the day was gone but the moon not yet out. The snow fell harder, the man pulled his sled, and the fox followed.

"The dark is too deep; you should stop or risk losing the path for good," said the fox.

The man said nothing. The snow was at his thighs now, crunching and parting as the man drove forward. The moon was rising.

"Just give up, man, rest! This may be your last chance," said the fox.

He paced quickly now through the drifts, his wild eyes set on the man.

The man said nothing, turning his gaze to the light ahead.

The fox was out of patience for his own game, and swiftly he made for the man's legs, clear atop the snow, but the man was on his step.

The fox looked up and met the dog.

For the Love of Mushrooms

Jack was going to die for some mushrooms.

He had been content gathering the abundant chanterelles in the area for the past two days, and there were three five-gallon buckets back at camp to attest to that! Although, it struck him now that he may never get to enjoy them: the storm had come in with such intensity that it had nearly taken the ground he was standing on away in a torrent of freezing wind and rain. Jack pressed on until the day began to fail, soaked to the bone and beaten. He fell where he stood and let the night come.

A light in the dark. Fire or some warmth through the trees, Jack was too desperate to wonder. Clambering to his feet, he stumbled forward over roots and rocks until the light was all around him. It was a cabin, old and traditional, and it looked like it was part of the forest. Jack climbed the stairs that lead inside with some difficulty; they were spaced apart much higher than he thought normal. The door was broad and tall with heavy iron bands and loops. Jack knocked.

There was no answer.

He knocked again, harder.

There was still no answer.

Jack tried the handle and to his surprise and relief it opened, though he struggled to push it. It seemed heavier than any door Jack had ever known.

The wind and the rain, lightning and thunder all buffeted the cabin, but Jack felt he was safe.

He looked around him.

The cabin was warmed by a bright stone hearth, wood still burning high. There were furs all about the place, and wildflowers and morels littered the counters and filled the room with the pungent and earthy tones of pine and truffle. All of the furniture was huge! Jack realized he would have had to climb into the nearest chair like a toddler. The kitchen was more of the same: a bread knife as big as sword, an icebox the size of a bedroom, and glasses and plates to match.

A smell hit Jack, dark and rich... a smell he knew yet could not describe completely, sweet like molasses and tangy like brown cheese. There was a plate set out on a table smaller than the rest of the room, and on it Jack found a cut of the darkest brown bread he had ever seen and a slab of butter amber yellow. Beside the plate sat a mug made of solid wood, with a liquid swirling inside that in one light looked like water and in another like gold, as Jack moved the mug, he thought a light had come from it like purest sunshine.

He set down his pack and reached within for his true bounty from the day, a dozen golden chanterelles. He placed them on the enormous main table as an offering to his hosts, whoever they were, and returned to his meal. The bread filled him with warmth and comfort, the drink tasted sweet and cool, it made him feel refreshed and at ease. Jack found a fur easily twice his size, heavy and black as pitch. He laid up near the hearth on the floor and let sleep and dreams take him.

Jack dreamed of giants, of a man bigger than reason moving about and singing lightly, the song somehow familiar. He dreamed of trees and flowers blooming, of roots sinking and searching, he dreamed of time passing and all things growing.

When Jack woke the storm had passed, the cabin was quiet and still. He cleaned his wares from dinner and set everything as back as it has been, as best he could, taking his time in hopes his host might return. Eventually he gathered his pack and opened the great main door to leave. He noticed the door felt a bit lighter, the steps not as steep. When Jack made it home all of his family and friends enjoyed the mushrooms he gathered, and they all thought he seemed a bit... taller. Every year he returns to the forest to gather mushrooms, and every year he leaves some at the step of the cabin.

Fire Eater

Reynar ran until his chest felt sure to burst. He was two hours past the wall, and from there the village was another hour north. He had started the day gathering what food he could find and checking the traps, but then the sky had turned an ominous green and bursts of roiling fire made a sound across the mountain so powerful he had fallen in fear. A ball of flame and colors tore the heavens apart, and Reynar watched in horror and awe as the star smote the mountain on its peak. The stones and earth seemed to dissolve into steam and ash, and a terrible cloud brought a sudden night. Despite all this chaos, Reynar ran straight towards the danger.

In the east valley, along the riverside, sat the village. The river flowed from the mountains, cold and clear as ice. When the blaze hit the mountain top it sent a rush of earth and timber down into the river below, the torrent raging downstream.

When Reynar reached the forests edge he could see the ruin, the village he had spent his whole life in, all he knew, was gone. There was nothing left, not a cabin or storehouse remained, it was dead quiet. He fell to his knees and wept, letting earth and darkness and grief overtake him.

Reynar woke in the night; it was pitch dark aside from an odd glow over the tops of the trees. He puzzled at it. At the river bank he could see what was left of the mountain: a haunted skeleton of remains, and on its jagged top was a light of colors beyond his reckoning. The light cast terrible and indelible shadows through the valley and over the now docile river. Foundations of stone and clay were all that remained of the village, and there was nothing here now but pain. Reynar looked at his hands for a long while, then at the light on the mountain. He stood.

Reynar set out with no plan or provisions, only with intent, to seek out the star on the mountain top and claim it as his own, if he could. As he followed the devastated banks of the river all manner of animals and beasts passed him by, all seeming to flee the calamity and the light the remained. The animals paid him no attention as they ran, even as Reynar had come upon a bear and her cubs and had expected a brutal ending, they moved past him as though he were a ghost.

Was he? Reynar wondered if he had died in the village too, died with his family at home and this was... something after. "No, you're here," Reynar said to himself as he bent to drink from the river. The water was frost cold and still muddy and dark, and a deep shiver rolled over him. After drinking his fill he rose and pushed on toward the mountain and the star. He walked for the whole of the light of day, and after night fell, he reached the fields where thick beds of grasses used to cover the earth; now there were boulders and rocks beyond counting.

That night Reynar rested, though the fire he made for warmth and comfort seemed to provide little of either, its light looking almost childish in the glow of the star. A night of wild dreams was only broken by the sounds of the forest around him, the garble of the river made the noises strange and Reynar did not trust his own senses. Sleep came in fits as he fed his fire and desperately tried not to think of home.

The sun rose pale and distant, and when it was fully light Reynar moved into the remains of the valley, now only a field of stone. Some of the stones were as big as a house, massive chunks of dark granite, but most others the size of acorns: an obliterated field of gravel, all of it with fresh, jagged edges. He was slow moving through the destruction, and by the steep end of the boulders he was crawling, his hands and feet torn and ragged. His strength dwindled to the last after that and he sat along the rim just below the summit. The dark was full again by then and there were no stars, at least not in the sky. The flaming jewel at the center of the crater, just in his view, was a burning, flowing light of every color thrown against the night, and it was warm even from this distance.

Reynar stood and listened hard; there was a sudden voice, a crackling and sharp voice just on the edge of hearing.

With the last draw of his strength Reynar made the summit, and he could see along the narrow ridge that remained that there was a deep depression, a molten cradle, and inside was the star.

Reynar was certain then; it was a star brought down from the night sky. It was the most beautiful and terrifying thing he had ever seen. The voice he had seemed to hear before was suddenly in his mind, a will that took him over almost entirely. He tried to resist it until the memory of the harsh fate behind him came back to his mind, and he moved forward.

Reynar approached the star; he looked at his ruined hands, then thrust them into the light. The heat was *immense*. The pain hit him all at once and the burning spread through his core. This was more pain than Reynar knew possible, and, steeling himself for an instant, he spoke.

"I accept." He pulled the star to his lips and ate it whole, even as the heat of it scorched his face. The pain reached a new high as the star burned deep down his throat and in his chest, then in an instant it was gone, and there was no pain, but a new sensation, trembling down his spine. He rose slowly, cautiously.

The first thing he noticed was the sky. He gasped. "So many stars!" His eyes fell to his hands, now new and whole.

The voice spoke. "Those? Those are not stars".

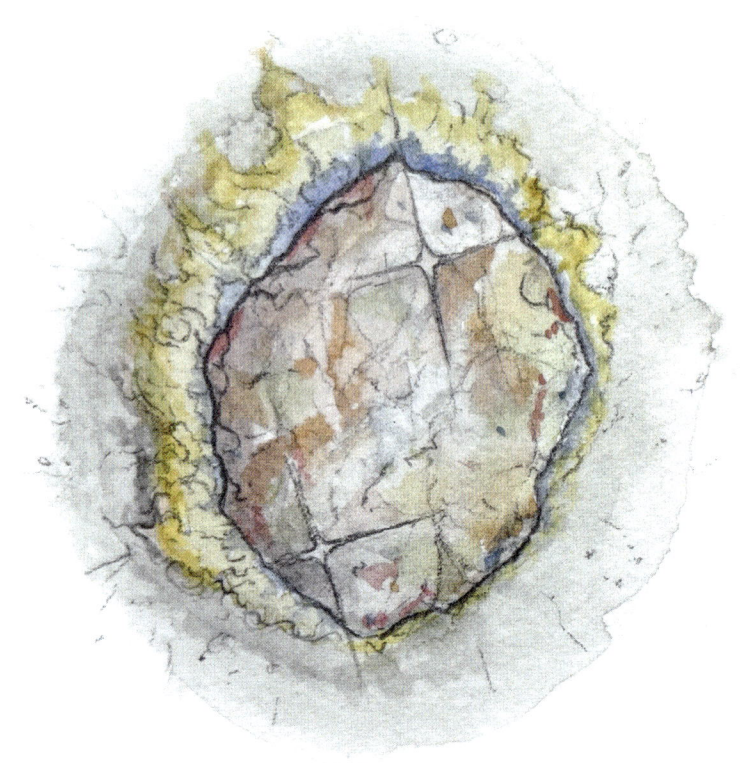

The Offering

There is a village not far from here, although you might not find it if you went looking. Only lost folk can find it, after a day of two in the woods they happen upon a stream, see a light in the distance, even smell some sweet aroma, all leading to the village. All kinds of lost folk wander in, hikers, campers, even foresters, all lost and all ending up set right again by the villagers, well, most all. It is said that after a meal in the circle and a good night's rest, the lost wake up and set out only to find they were just off the trails, though they can never find the place again.

There is a cost for the lost to be found

and the found to stay lost.

The sun was setting and Emma was waking up, again. She couldn't sleep at night out here, too many sounds. Her fire was getting low and she knew she was out of wood to burn. It had been two days since she lost the trail. Emma had only meant to use the bathroom, just off the path, and now she was out of food and water, facing another nine hours of night.

"Just breathe," Emma said. She was sure that the next morning someone would be looking for her, if they weren't already.

The fire popped as the flames broke to glowing embers and the night set in. The dark was full and deep, and Emma could see no stars or moon in the sky above, just a low blanket of clouds scraping the treetops like a fog. She focused on the fluttering remains of the dying fire as the forest came alive around her. Odd sounds cracked and groaned in the night, each making her drowsing eyes flutter open again and dart around in confusion. As the embers turned ashen and the dark moved in on her, Emma stared at the forest around, never quite catching a good look at the sources of the snaps and groans that stalked the shadows of the trees.

In the pitch then, at the very edge of her view, a light jumped into life; like a torchlight off in the forest it emanated a soft glow that seemed to pour into her. Emma took a deep breath, gathering the reserves of her will to pull herself off the ground, and set out towards the light. She stumbled through the trees, brushing aside the wet branches of pines and trying to keep her soaked boots beneath her.

The torch was closer than she thought; it stood in a clearing with a path winding up a hill around the sprawl of dense trees. The thick wood of the torch itself was beyond ornate, carved deeply and with a fine mahogany finish that was unblemished. Runes ran along it like words on pages, and Emma felt as if she could read them, though she couldn't understand.

She could see there was another torch burning brightly past the first, along a path that was barely more than a game trail. She moved to it as if in a dream, pushing off into the woods.

As she reached the next torch, and the next, Emma noticed them beginning to wear, their fine runes becoming rough and worn, the metal sconces that held them twisting and rusting with age. The path wound into a valley, torches standing every so often to make clear the way. Her boots stumbled across a makeshift bridge and splashed through an icy brook that babbled with a strange sound. Her feet suddenly found the rough, cobbled stones of a path that seemed to grow from the forest floor. She could finally see the dim outline of a village through the trees ahead.

The path led her through a high arch of living trees, and as she passed under their woven branches, Emma glanced wearily at the sky above. The inky, starless expanse seemed to peer back. Emma drew a deep, shuddering breath and made her way through the dark towards the cabins ahead. A dull horror stirred in her throat as she realized each of their shutters were drawn tight, and the only light around her was from the line of ancient torches. Desperately, Emma pushed open the gate to the first house on the path and made for its dark door. She beat her fist against its worn wood but stopped just as suddenly: the sound felt like a violation of the silence surrounding her.

Emma thought she could hear footsteps in the cabin approaching the door, but it did not open. She tried to yell out but found it impossible.

As Emma continued down the path in a daze, she glanced at each cabin for any sign of mercy. Finding none in their shadowy sills, she followed the light of the torches. The last cabin in the village was set back from the path, nestled deep against the very foot of the mountain. As she approached its gate, she barely looked at the fastened windows, for she knew they were dark and hopeless. But when she pushed the gate open, she saw a small basket of apples resting there on the stoop. An offering?

Her breath hitched in her chest as she lunged forward towards them, sinking against the rough-hewn wood of the door and pulling the basket into her lap. She grabbed one and bit into it, ravenous. They were the best apples she had even known, reds, greens, and yellows all crisp and ripe to perfection.

After having her fill, Emma lifted her heavy eyes to the last torch of the street in front of her. The blurry thought to rest there filled her mind, under the light of the torch. This last torch was of the same wood as the first, but so much older; the colors and textures of time made it look more like stone, though its runes were just as clear. As she stared, the jagged symbols began to glow with a deep and distant fire, dancing against the mountain and revealing the mouth of a cave at the end of the path before her. It beckoned her into is depths.

 In the cave, the dark was alive, the way down was straight and steep. The air had grown colder and stale, there was a growing feeling of control and dread to every step she took into the mountain. The sounds of the earth shifting and straining, water finding ways through the rock, icy air filling the space around her, all made Emma feel like she was in the oldest part of the world. It was as if nothing loved her there.

Suddenly the dark was punctuated by a growing dot of light further down the tunnel, and after what seemed like hours the path opened wide, to a space like a cathedral of stone, with a glowing ring of ancient torches standing in the middle. Along all the walls, covering every surface, there were runes carved deep in the stone, and they all burned with that same distant fire. She had felt it then, a sudden chill and the knowing feeling, that something was there with her, watching. The torches seemed to react to the presence, guttering and flaring, throwing shadows all about the room. Emma approached the center of the ring, her body really and truly no longer her own. The rising shadows ran together as one, the torches flashed then as they gave way to the dark, and the beastly form it had chosen. It enveloped her with inky blackness and she knew no more.

In the village, the torches all went out, the stars and moon came back into the night, and all the shutters of the cabins drew open with a single, quiet motion.

The Inkwell

The inkwell was at the center, in the valley, both below and above; the paper gave way to dye, viscous and abyss. The page was blank, hues of vanilla and amber patched together in perfect disorder, the edges smoldering and ashen as embers spit off in the void. The inkwell sat upon the page, unfathomable depths of deepest dark contained in and of it. The well cracked, the ink was free, and the world was shaped. Mountains, lakes, valleys, oceans, forests, and the spaces between, all bled into existence as the font flowed loose. Imperfections and coincidence give the land its magic. Deepest black for the waters, peaks of snow-white mountains, forests that ran to the burning edges of the world, and in the center was the inkwell.

There is no pen, never was, and all that the things that love and loathe came from the ink and the paper, the between where union and chance made possible. The first was Woman.

From the forests she was born and, in the forests, she kept the embers at bay. When time began in the world the woman began to wonder and want. She looked anew at the embers, their golden reds and bursts of yellow and orange were more than she had considered. She took an ember in her smooth hand and gave life to it; wisdom came to her then and counseled she take the ember to the inkwell, though she did not know then if this was salvation or doom. The ember spoke to her then: if she wanted to take it so far, she would have to make an offering. In this beginning Woman had two minds and two hearts, and so she offered one of each to the ember. With a heart and a mind, ember became flame, which Woman could carry to the well. As she traveled from the edges and forests, flame cast shadows all about that jumped and danced in the light and into life themselves, monstrous and strange, shadows of life that depend on and despise the light altogether.

The forests were alive then, as she traveled from the wood to the mountains and into the valleys below, the shadows following close. Woman swam in the oceans, peering into their dark and wild depths. Her feet broke over peaks of snow and raging wind, and with flame in her hands she came to a valley, barren and vast. In its center was the well.

She brought forward flame and set it at the edge, set him, and he stood then as man both of flesh and flame. He looked into the inkwell and reached forth with a hand wreathed in fire, the other hand was in hers and she was of earth and soil. Where the fire met the ink color issued forth, flowing unending beyond the void. The world filled with life, flora and fauna beyond recount both foul and fair.

Roots grew where she held him, across and into the well, all about them and deep into the page, a tree grew. Its roots were the roots of the earth, and at the roots she held him, earth and flame, holding the world itself. The canopy covered the valley in leaves of eternal autumn, golden reds and bursts of yellow and orange.

The tree bore two fruits, the first was a man both severe and comforting, unfamiliar and unmistakable, he was Thought. The second was a woman, fickle and generous, empathetic and uncaring, she was Muse. They were color.

The shadows scattered and fled; they abhor the colors more than any light, they dug deep into the page hiding themselves away until the flame falls.

Thank you, to my friends and family that supported my education, parenting, and writing. *More to come*

Michael Eska – *RithÖfundur (Author)*

Ophia – *Editor and Illustrator*

Made in the USA
Las Vegas, NV
29 March 2022